Disney Girls

And Sleepy Makes Seven

Gabrielle Charbonnet

Disney
PRESS

NEW YORK

Printed in the United States of America.

First Edition

3   5   7   9   10   8   6   4

The text of this book is set in 15-point Adobe Garamond.

Library of Congress Catalog Card Number: 98-84796

ISBN: 0-7868-4158-3

For more Disney Press fun, visit www.DisneyBooks.com

Contents

Disney Girls

And Sleepy Makes Seven

Chapter One

Twice the Fun

"Wow, those are cool barrettes," my friend Ariel Ramos said to me. "They look like real pearls."

The first morning bell was about to ring. Our third-grade teacher, Ms. Timmons, walked into our class-room with her book bag over her shoulder. She smiled at us.

I flipped back my shoulder-length black hair with my hand. "Thanks," I said. "I got them last weekend at Accessories. Mom and I went shopping for some baby things."

"Did you get anything fun?" asked Ella O'Connor.

"Some really cute bibs and these weensy baby socks," I said, pinching my fingers together to show how small. "They looked like socks for a cat."

Ariel and Ella laughed. Ariel is one of my best friends. Ella is my *absolutely* best friend. My name is Yukiko Hayashi. We're all in third grade at Orlando Elementary, in Orlando, Florida.

So far, third grade is turning out to be a lot like I thought it would be. It's harder than second grade. We have homework more often. And we're learning about more interesting things. Mostly, I feel older, being a third grader. Like I'm not a little kid anymore.

Once the bell rang, the three of us sat down at our desks. I wish we sat next to each other, but we don't. At least we're all in Ms. Timmons's room. Our school has two third-grade classes, and we could have been split up.

This morning, our teacher quickly called the roll. Ms. Timmons is nice, but she can be kind of strict. Already this year she had sent Malcolm and Peter to the principal's office for what they had done with the paste pots.

After roll call, Ms. Timmons stood at the front of our room. "Class, I have an exciting announcement," she said. "You all know Halloween is on Friday of next week. Usually each class has its own Halloween party."

Ella and I gave each other a thumbs-up. We love class parties.

"This year, Mr. Murchison, who teaches fourth grade across the hall, and I have decided to combine our two classes and have a party together."

My eyebrows raised, and I glanced over at Ella and Ariel.

"All right!" said Ariel, punching the air.

This was so cool! Ariel, Ella, and I have three other best friends: Paula Pinto, Isabelle Beaumont, and Jasmine Prentiss. They're all in Mr. Murchison's class. This announcement meant the six of us would be together for the Halloween class party! It would be twice as much fun!

Ms. Timmons held up her hand for silence. "I'd like to take ten minutes before class begins to write down some party ideas on the board. Think about refreshments, dec-orations, music, games—anything that will make our party a success. Please remember to raise your hands."

Instantly hands shot up all over the classroom—but not mine. I never raise my hand in class. With my friends I'm friendly and talk a lot, but in front of groups of people—

even kids—I don't even like to open my mouth! I hardly ever give an answer unless Ms. Timmons asks me to.

"Let's have popcorn balls!" said Barclay Forbes.

"I have a CD of Halloween songs," Rebecca James said.

"Let's bob for apples!" Ariel called, waving her hand. "We could get a big tub of water. . . ."

"That might be a little messy for class," Ms. Timmons said with a smile. "But thanks for the idea."

Ella raised her hand, too. "We could drink witch's brew. I have a recipe."

Ms. Timmons wrote everything down on the blackboard. It sounded like we were going to have the best Halloween party ever! Maybe I could make pumpkin-shaped cookies for the party. I already knew what costume I would wear: my really fancy Snow White dress. Ella would be wearing her Cinderella ball gown, and Ariel would be dressed as the Little Mermaid, of course.

Just then a folded note landed on my desk. I looked up to see Ariel grinning at me. When Ms. Timmons turned around to write more suggestions on the board, Ariel lobbed a note at Ella. It fell right into her lap.

I put my note under my desk and opened it. Ariel *knows* we're not supposed to pass notes in class. She's really daring that way. I wish I could be. I'm always too afraid I'd get caught.

My note said:

Another Brilliant Idea by Ariel. This is perfect! We'll all be in costume! Everyone come to my house after school! We'll hang out, eat dinner, go trick-or-treating together! Then we'll have a fantabulous Disney Girls sleep-over! We'll eat all our candy! We'll have a great time! Talk to you later!

                                   -Love, Ariel

It sounded great—nothing is more fun than a Disney Girls sleepover. (I'll explain about the Disney Girls in a minute.) And it made sense to go right from school to Ariel's house. There was only one problem: I hadn't been trick-or-treating since I was five years old—and I wasn't sure I wanted to go this year. But what would Ariel, Ella, and the others say if I didn't want to trick-or-treat with them? Would they think I was totally uncool?

I hid the note in my desk. I met Ariel's eyes and gave her a small thumbs-up. I would just have to figure it out later.

5

Chapter Two

My Family Away from My Family

Today I had brought my lunch from home, so I skipped the cafeteria line and went to our usual table. Soon my friends and I were sitting with our food spread out in front of us.

"What's that, Yukiko?" asked Jasmine, peering into my Tupperware containers.

"Leftover Japanese food from last night. My mom's been craving it lately," I explained. I'm American, and so are my mom and my stepdad. But their parents were from Japan. So we like to keep in touch with our Japanese heritage.

"How much longer till the baby gets here?" asked Isabelle.

I took a sip of milk. "Four weeks." My mom is going to have a baby soon—around the middle of November. (That's why we had gone shopping.) I was really, really hoping it would be a girl, because I already have *six* brothers.

"Anyone want some cheese puffs?" asked Ariel.

Paula made a face. "Ariel, those are full of artificial coloring and flavoring."

"That's what makes 'em taste so good," said Ariel, crunching happily.

Sometimes it's hard to believe, but Ariel and Paula are best friends—even though they're pretty different. Actually, the six of us are all best friends—*and* we're also three pairs of *really* best friends: me and Ella, Ariel and Paula, and Jasmine and Isabelle.

Ella and I met way back in preschool. We lived close to each other, in Willow Hill, which is a neighborhood in Orlando. As soon as Ella and I met, we knew we were meant to be friends. We're both shy around strangers, we both love to play dress-up and pretend, and we both love cats and chocolate-dipped pretzels and watermelon-flavored lip gloss. Ella was the sister I didn't have.

Then, in kindergarten, Ella and I met Ariel. Ariel was already best friends with Paula, who lived around the corner from her. Paula was in first grade. It wasn't long before the four of us were inseparable. That's when we first realized what was so incredible about our friendship. That's when we realized that we were Disney Girls.

It's hard to explain exactly what a Disney Girl is. It's not official or anything—it's just what we call ourselves. And it's not something we planned or made up. It just *is*.

One rainy afternoon at Paula's, the four of us gathered to watch the movie *Pocahontas*. Of course we had all seen it at the movie theater, but we were so excited to see it again on video.

The more we watched the movie, the more the air in the room seemed to tingle. The more we saw Pocahontas on the screen, the more familiar she seemed to us. I blinked, and instead of Pocahontas running across the screen, it was Paula! I blinked again and it was Pocahontas. I sat up and rubbed my eyes, then glanced across at Ella. She looked thoughtful. I looked at my other friends, then we all stared at Paula.

"What?" she said. "Was I singing along again? Sorry."

"Paula," I said slowly. "It's *you*."

"Yeah," Ella whispered. She put her hand to her cheek. "I saw it, too."

"Oh, my gosh," said Ariel. "Are you guys saying what I think you're saying? Are you saying Paula looks like Pocahontas?"

I shook my head. "Not just *looks* like," I said. *"Is."*

Paula sat up and hit the pause button on the VCR. "It is *so* weird that you guys said that," she began. Then it all came out. "I have this magical connection with Pocahontas," Paula explained. "As if I really *am* her. Everything Pocahontas says or does, I could say or do the same thing! It's like looking into a mirror."

We sat there, trying to take this in. Then I said, "Wow, you guys. I can't believe this—but you know the movie *Snow White*?"

"No duh," said Ariel. "Of course we do."

"Well, even though I don't look exactly like her, I still feel like her," I admitted. "It's like I'm looking at myself when I watch that movie. Even my name, Yukiko, means 'snow child' in Japanese. I have only three little brothers, but they remind me of the Dwarfs. I mean, I just *am* Snow White."

(I told you I have six brothers. Right after the twins,

9

Kazuo and Nobuo, were born, my dad died. A year and a half later, my mom met Jim Hayashi, my stepfather. He was divorced, with three boys of his own. When he and Mom got married, he adopted my brothers and me, so we all have the same last name. Back in kindergarten, though, it was just me, my mom, and my three brothers.)

"Oh, my gosh, this is almost spooky," said Ariel. "I mean, look at *this*. Remind you of anyone?" She held up her *Little Mermaid* backpack and pointed to the picture. We all looked from the picture to her and back again.

"We both have long red hair and blue eyes," said Ariel. "We both love to swim. We both have a bunch of sisters. We even have the same name! When I saw *The Little Mermaid* movie, I thought they had sneaked a video camera into my house and filmed me!"

"Except you don't live under the ocean," Ella joked.

"No, but I could," said Ariel. She frowned. "I would. If I had gills."

Whoa. We all felt strange, as if we had stepped into a new universe. We looked at each other again and again. Now I easily saw Pocahontas's eyes looking out of Paula's face. Now it seemed almost odd that Ariel had legs and feet instead of a tail.

On cue, the three of us turned to stare at Ella.

She grinned and blushed a little bit. "It's true," she said. "I'm Cinderella. Cinder*ella.* Get it?"

Back then, Ella's father hadn't gotten remarried yet. It was just the two of them. But she was Cinderella, all right. You could see it just by looking at her. She had felt it the first time she saw her movie.

From then on, our friendships became even deeper. A new, magical world opened up to us. The more we felt like ourselves (our *real* selves) the more magic we could see everywhere, in everything. That was when we started making magic wishes.

The next year, when I was six, my mom married Jim. (Which brought the number of Dwarfs up to six.) Then last year I met Jasmine in my ballet class. The more I talked to her, the more I got a familiar feeling about her. One day, months later, she confided in me about how she felt about the movie *Aladdin.* I brought her to my house to meet Ariel, Paula, and Ella. That's how Jasmine became the fifth Disney Girl—Princess Jasmine.

Last summer, Ella's dad married a woman with two daughters. So far, they really do seem like Cinderella's stepmother and stepsisters. But maybe things will get better soon.

11

Finally, just a few weeks ago, Isabelle transferred to our school. She and Jasmine hit it off right away. For a while we were worried that Jasmine might choose being friends with Isabelle over being a Disney Girl. It all worked out, though. Isabelle is Belle, from *Beauty and the Beast!*

Magic brought us all together. Now we make magic happen in our lives. And that's why we're the Disney Girls.

Chapter Three

Back to the Zoo

"Ooof!" My breath got knocked out of me as I stepped off the school bus. "Watch it!" I yelled at my brothers Ben and Yoshi. They pounded up our walk ahead of me, not caring that they had smushed me like a pancake against the school bus door.

My friends had already been dropped off at their houses. (Jasmine lives in a fancy suburb called Wildwood Estates. Her mother usually picks her up from school.) Ben, Yoshi, and I are usually the last kids on the bus.

I used my key to let us in, and the boys thundered to the

kitchen. Inside, I waved out the window to my mom, who was in the backyard with my youngest brother, Daniel.

"Please!" Ben gasped, screeching to a halt. He clutched my arm and slid to the floor. "Drink! Please!" He lay on the floor, holding his throat and coughing as if he was lost in the desert. Then his eyes rolled into the back of his head and he flopped a little like a fish. "Gaaack," he said weakly.

I sighed. Yoshi giggled. Quickly I poured three iced teas.

"Want this?" I asked Ben loudly. I held it above him and pretended to almost pour it on him. He opened one eye. I let the glass tip a little more. One drop ran over the edge and splatted on his forehead.

"Hey!" He leaped up and grabbed the glass.

I grinned. "Glad to see you recovered." I fixed us all graham crackers with cream cheese. Ben and Yoshi snatched theirs as if they had been raised by wolves and ran out into the backyard. I decided to fix my mom a snack, too, and brought it out to her.

"Hi, Mom!" I called, walking across the lawn.

"Thank you, sweetheart," Mom said, biting into a graham cracker. "That was thoughtful of you."

14

I patted her round tummy. "How's my little sister today?"

"He or she is fine," my mom said, smiling.

Daniel came over and pointed to my cracker. He's three years old, but doesn't talk much. He reminds me of Dopey, the little Dwarf. I shared my cracker with him.

"Hey!" yelled Yoshi. "Cut it out! I had it first!"

"It's mine, you weiner!" Ben shouted back. "No fair!"

Mom and I looked up to see the boys each grabbing an end of a big water-soaker water gun. Ben ripped it out of Yoshi's hands and they started chasing each other, running in circles around our wishing well. (It isn't a real well. Maybe it used to be, a long time ago. Now it's filled with dirt and has flowers planted in it. Sometimes, when I really need magic's help, I make wishes by it.)

To fill you in on the Dwarfs, Ben is seven, one year younger than me. He's Doc, because he's the oldest boy and a little bossy. Then there's Yoshi, who's six now. He's Bashful—at least around strangers. Michael is five. He has allergies, so he's Sneezy. The twins, Kazuo and Nobuo, are next. They're four years old. Although they look identical, Kazuo is Grumpy (boy, is he!) and Nobuo is Happy. He's never in a bad mood. It makes it easy to tell them apart. Then Daniel is Dopey.

My mom and dad had given us all Japanese names. (My mom's name is Masako.) Jim and his wife had given their boys American names. But now we're all Hayashis, all together. Soon our family would be even bigger: we were going to have a new baby (please let it be a girl!), and my mom's parents were coming to live with us. In fact, Jim was building on two more rooms to our house, so that Grandma and Grandpa would have their own space. They were selling their house in Miami.

"No name-calling, please," Mom said, and took another bite of her cracker.

"We're going to have a Halloween party at school," I told her. Yoshi caught up to Ben and managed to grab the water-soaker. Ben howled in anger. They started running again, and Yoshi almost tripped over Mom's potted rosemary plant.

"That sounds fun," said Mom.

"Can we make pumpkin-shaped cookies?" I asked.

"Sure. Guys, how about taking turns?" The boys acted like they hadn't heard her. Daniel reached for another cracker.

"Hi, all!" called Jim, stepping out the back door. He had the twins and Michael with him—they'd had play dates this afternoon. They saw Ben and Yoshi running, and they started running after them. The water-soaker was forgotten and the five of them started playing freeze tag.

"Ha! You're it, skeezeball!" taunted Michael as he tapped Yoshi on the shoulder.

"No name-calling," Mom repeated.

Jim came over and kissed me and Mom. "How are you feeling?" he asked Mom.

She smiled. "Tired, but fine."

"What do you feel like having for dinner?" he asked.

Mom thought. "A Grand Happy Jack Burger?"

Jim laughed. "With extra fries?"

"Yes," said Mom. "Is that okay?"

"Sure. The kids will love it. I'll go get it in a while." Jim sat next to Mom on the grass. The three of us watched the boys run around like chickens with their heads cut off. I really love Jim. He acts like my real father. I'm glad we're a family.

Just then Kazuo took a sudden turn and barreled right into me from behind.

"Ahh!" I screamed, landing right on my face. My iced tea flew out of my hand, spraying Mom and Jim. Kazuo

17

landed on top of me, then bounced off my back. My glass rolled under our hydrangea bush. Kazuo leaped up and rejoined the game of tag. "Be careful, you idiot!" I yelled. Slowly I picked myself up and brushed dirt and grass off my knees and dress.

"No name-calling," Mom reminded me, dabbing at her wet dress with a napkin. "You okay?"

I glared at my brothers with narrowed eyes. "You better have a girl this time," I told Mom.

"I'll try, honey," Mom promised.

I turned around and stomped toward the house. "I'm going inside, where it's a little safer," I said.

"I'll let you know when dinner's here," Jim called after me.

Inside, I slammed the door to my room, and that helped me feel a little better. I changed out of my ruined dress. Sometimes the other DGs tease me because I like to wear kind of frilly, girly clothes. But I just don't like wearing jeans or T-shirts. That's what my *brothers* wear. *I* like Laura Ashley. Even my whole room is done like Laura Ashley. The more lace and ruffles, the better, is the way I see it.

I flopped down on my bed and looked around my

room. Ben and Yoshi share a room, and so do Michael and Kazuo, and Nobuo and Daniel. If the new baby was a girl, I would share my room with her. If the new baby was a boy, he'd go in with Nobuo and Daniel.

I figured I could push my bed closer to the wall to make room for a crib. I could empty out two of my dresser drawers to make room for baby clothes. I wouldn't mind.

If the new baby was a girl, I would finally have a sister. I wouldn't be the only girl. A sister would like to play the kind of games I like to play. She wouldn't constantly be screaming and fighting and yelling and breaking things. She would be an ally. Two girls against six boys still wasn't even, but it was better than one against seven. "Please let the baby be a girl," I whispered. "I'll do anything."

Chapter Four

Pocahontas

On Wednesday morning, Ariel bounded onto the school bus. She spotted Ella, Isabelle, and me, and waved. Paula filed on after her, and they took the seats we had saved for them.

"Guess what!" Ariel said, dropping her backpack to the floor. "I asked Mom and Dad, and they said we could have the sleepover! Cool, huh?"

"That's great!" said Ella. "It'll be so fun. I love sleep-overs at your house."

Ariel grinned. "What should we do to my sisters *this*

time?" Ariel likes to play practical jokes on her three sisters. I have to admit, it's fun.

"My mom brought home a ginormous plastic pumpkin for me to trick-or-treat with," said Isabelle. "I bet it gets filled up to the top. Last year I actually had to go home halfway through, just to dump out my bag."

"Wow," said Ella. She bounced a little on our seat and smiled at me. "I can't wait!"

I managed a little smile back.

"Okay, so you guys will all come home with me after school," Ariel directed. "You'll need notes from your moms to give to Mrs. Holiday." Mrs. Holiday is our school bus driver. "We'll have dinner, then hit the streets with my dad."

"You know," said Paula, "this will be the first year that we'll go trick-or-treating together, the six of us."

"That's right," Ella said. She turned to me. "Last year you were away on vacation."

"Yes," I said. "We were in Japan. And the year before that, Mom and Jim were on their honeymoon. I was in Miami."

"Now we have Isabelle, too," Paula pointed out. "Our group is complete. This will be a super-fantastic Halloween."

I nodded, but I didn't feel that way. The last time I had gone trick-or-treating, I had gotten lost in the dark. I know it sounds kind of silly, but I was only five years old, and it had been scary. And it made me not feel like trying it again. But how could I tell my friends without sounding like a baby? Maybe I could get out of it. . . .

"You know," I said, "sometimes I wonder if trick-or-treating is really that great. I bet if we had a sleepover at Ariel's house and *didn't* go trick-or-treating, I would have just as much fun. We'd have a terrific *party*. . . ." I trailed off as I noticed four pairs of eyes staring at me in disbelief.

"Not go trick-or-treating?" Ariel practically shrieked. "Are you *crazy*?"

"You mean, not go at *all*?" Ella asked, her eyes wide.

My cheeks grew warm with embarrassment. "Never mind," I mumbled. "Just a thought. I didn't mean it."

"Gee, I *always* go trick-or-treating," Isabelle said mildly.

"Yeah, forget it," I said. "It'll be great." *Not*, I thought.

On Saturday, Paula invited us all over to play at her house. She has a great backyard. It's really big, and she has three huge old willow trees in it. She also has a tree house, big enough to hold all of us! It used to be her brother

Damon's, but he doesn't play in it anymore. (He's in ninth grade, and is really cool.)

Today everyone was already in the yard when I rode my bike up. Since we were at Paula's house, we were all members of Pocahontas's tribe. It's one of the things we do—take turns acting out each other's lives as Disney princesses. When we're swimming with Ariel, we're all mermaids. At Paula's we're all Native Americans. It's a blast.

I waved my arm in a salute. "Wing-gap-o," I said, which means "Hello."

"Wing-gap-o," said Ella, looking up. She was pounding on a brick with another brick.

"What are you doing?" I asked.

"Gathering the harvest. Winter will be here soon."

Paula's yard also has a couple of pecan trees in it. Every other year, her yard is carpeted with pecans. Today my friends were gathering them. Ella was cracking one open with a brick. Once it popped open, she picked out the nut and ate it.

"Hey!" said Ariel. "Save some for winter, okay?"

Ella smiled guiltily. "Sorry, Nakoma."

Paula's parents also have a large vegetable patch in their

backyard. (They're vegetarians.) Paula and Isabelle were in the vegetable patch, pulling weeds.

"Want a carrot?" Isabelle asked, gently tugging one out of the ground.

"Sure," I said. I washed it off under the hose and ate it. It was delicious. Then I got to work, to help my tribe prepare for winter. I fetched water in buckets, climbed up to the tree house to make sure the white savages weren't sneaking up on us, and tried to make arrows out of some long sticks. We dug in the dirt, played with Meeko (he's Paula's pet raccoon—a real raccoon!), and swept out the tree house.

Later, right before we had to go home for dinner, we all lay on our backs in the grass and looked up at the sky.

"I see a beautiful castle," said Jasmine.

"There's a great big ship, with sails," Ariel pointed out.

"I see a new baby sister," I said.

"Does your mom know if it's a boy or a girl?" Ella asked eagerly, sitting up.

I shook my head. "She's having an ultrasound soon. They might be able to tell then. I don't know, you guys." I bit my thumbnail. "I am just so afraid it's going to be a boy. I mean, I love my brothers—usually. But I just can't handle another horrible boy. I think I would have to run away from home."

"I don't blame you," said Ella.

"Maybe we should make a magic wish," suggested Isabelle.

"Great idea," I said. We all linked pinkies and quietly chanted:

All the magic powers that be,
Hear us now, our special plea.
Yukiko's head is in a whirl.
Please help her baby be a girl.

I felt better when I rode my bike home for dinner. The magic had never let me down yet. In fact, right then there was only one little thing bothering me: I still hadn't told my friends I didn't want to go trick-or-treating.

Chapter Five

At Home with the Dwarfs

On Sunday my family and I worked in the garden. Jim is an architect (he designed our house), and he also loves to design gardens. He's turning our plain backyard into a beautiful oasis. Today he asked us all to help him get the garden ready for fall.

"I know it's only October," he said with a smile. "But soon it will be December and autumn will be here."

We laughed. In Orlando, we basically have seven months of summer, four months of autumn, and one month of spring. Spring happens in March—then, *boom!* It's over.

Yoshi and I always like working in the garden. We sat

side by side, pulling weeds in our own small vegetable patch, which isn't nearly as big as the Pintos'. I thought again how Yoshi really is Bashful. He hates talking to strangers. It takes him a long time to open up to someone. But I understand how he feels and we get along well.

Ben was trying to get Daniel and the twins to help him move a small pile of rocks. "Come on, guys," he said. "Load them into the wagon, okay?" He pointed to our big green wagon. Nobuo scooped up some rocks and tried to dump them in the wagon, but he bumped into Kazuo by accident.

"Watch it, dumbhead!" Kazuo snapped. He picked up some rocks and flung them at Nobuo. A few hit him, but some whizzed past him and almost broke our kitchen window.

"Kazuo!" Jim said firmly. "Time out!" He pointed to a chair.

Nobuo burst into tears. I went over and patted his shoulder till he stopped.

"Ah-choo!" Michael started sneezing from being around all the plants.

"Inside, Michael, and ask your mother for your medicine," Jim directed.

When I looked up again, Daniel had disappeared. We dropped everything and searched for him. We couldn't find him for a long time until we thought to look behind the compost pile.

That's what life is like in my family all the time.

After lunch, Mom needed to rest for a while. I got the Dwarfs together around our dining room table. (Our table is Japanese-style, which means it is very low to the ground. We sit on pillows on the floor to eat. All my friends love it. Jim likes it because it honors our Japanese heritage. Mom thinks it's good because it's the right height for little kids. We don't have high chairs or boosters or kids falling off chairs and making a mess.)

Anyway. I had been thinking of something we could all do together for the baby. I set out poster boards, scissors, markers, and piles of stickers.

"Listen, you guys," I said. "We're going to do an art project for the new baby. We have a big, confusing family, and the baby will need all the help it can get. We're going to make a photo album of our family."

I showed them how to cut out a picture-frame shape. Each of us would decorate one, then put a photo in it.

"Remember to put your name on your frame, so the

baby will know who you are," I instructed. "We'll also make frames for Mom and Dad and Grandma and Grandpa and Grammy."

(When we kids are all together, we always just say Mom and Dad. Actually, everyone calls my mom Mom, because Ben, Michael, and Daniel never see their mom anymore. The twins call Jim Dad, because they don't remember our real dad. Yoshi and I usually call him Jim, but lately I had heard Yoshi call him Dad a few times. I was thinking about trying it myself.)

For a while we worked on our frames. It was fun having all of us doing something together. I was helping Daniel cut out his frame when Kazuo threw down his scissors.

"I can't do this," he said grumpily. "These dumb scissors don't work."

"Are you using the left-handed ones Mom got you?" I asked. "With the red handles?"

"No," Kazuo admitted. "I couldn't find them."

So I had to drop everything and go find Kazuo's southpaw scissors, and while I was gone Daniel cut his frame in half by accident and started crying, then Nobuo and Michael got into a wrestling match over the purple marker and knocked the whole box of markers to the floor, which made Ben angry so he kicked them, so everyone yelled and threw pillows at him.

I was gone for two seconds. I came back to total chaos.

"Hold it!" I shouted, waving my arms. My brothers kept yelling and chasing and crying and throwing stuff. I thought about how wonderful it would be when I could have quiet little tea parties with my new sister.

I shouted again, but the Dwarfs ignored me. Finally I picked up our big dictionary and dropped it to the floor.

Wham!

The Dwarfs froze.

"Here! Take these!" I practically shoved Kazuo's scissors into his hands. Then I grabbed Nobuo by his shirt and plunked him at one end of the table. I sat Daniel at the other. Ben put the pillows back in place, then picked up the markers while I repaired Daniel's frame with tape.

"Now everyone be quiet and sit down," I snapped. "We're supposed to be having fun!" My brothers finally settled down and went back to work.

I made my frame pink, and scalloped the edges. I wrote my name in fancy curlicue letters. Then I put flower and heart stickers all over it. Next I cut out a white frame for the baby. I handed it around to my brothers so they could each add a decoration.

I had almost finished Mom's frame when the baby's frame got back to me. I stared at it in horror. Each one of the Dwarfs had decorated it for a *boy*. There were football stickers, race cars, trucks, and male action figures.

"You guys," I cried, "what if the baby is a girl?"

My brothers stared at me silently for a moment. Then they burst into laughter.

"A *girl*?" asked Michael. He sneezed. "It won't be a girl."

"Mom and Dad wouldn't know what to do with a girl," said Yoshi. He glanced at me quickly and said, "A *baby* girl, that is."

"Of course it's going to be another boy," said Ben confidently.

"The. New. Baby. Will. Be. A. Girl," I said through gritted teeth. "Get. Used. To. It."

I glared at them for a moment, then pulled out a roll of stickers. I covered that frame with hearts, flowers, little animals, and butterflies.

Chapter Six

A Disney Girl Surprise

"Yukiko?" Mom called me late that afternoon. "Phone for you."

I ran to the phone in the kitchen. "Hello?"

"Hi," said Ella. "Are you busy?"

"Not right now," I said. I filled her in on my day, and she laughed. She's used to my brothers.

"I'm over at Ariel's," Ella said. "Can you come over? Ariel wants to plan the sleepover."

"I probably can," I said. "I'll see you soon."

A few minutes later, I parked my bike around the back

of Ariel's house. Mrs. Ramos let me in the kitchen door. She has bright red hair, like Ariel. Dr. Ramos and Ariel's sisters all have dark hair.

As I trotted upstairs, I thought about the sleepover. It would be our usual fabulous Disney Girls good time, I knew. If only I could get out of going trick-or-treating somehow! Maybe a brilliant idea would come to me.

I opened Ariel's door.

"Surprise!" the Disney Girls yelled. I leaped back, my heart pounding. Ariel took my arm and pulled me into her room.

"Surprise," she said again.

"What's going on?" I asked in bewilderment.

"It's a baby shower!" said Ella.

I was confused. "Shouldn't my mom be here?"

"We decided to have one just for you," Paula explained. "We thought maybe it would cheer you up about the baby."

"Wow—just for me? Great!" I said happily. "You're the best!"

"We know," said Ariel airily. "Look, we have some yummy eats."

Piled on her desk were cupcakes, glasses of punch,

dishes of candy, a bowl of popcorn, and a bag of chips.

"Yum!" I took a cupcake and peeled off the paper. "Fantastic! This is just what I needed," I said, taking a bite.

"Face it," said Isabelle. "Cupcakes are what *everyone* needs." We all laughed.

We descended on the food like sharks attacking a school of fish. While we ate I looked around Ariel's room to see if she had done anything new. She's always changing something. My room has stayed almost the same since we moved in two years ago, but Ariel's room seems different practically every week. She calls it her grotto.

Her room is just like her: kind of wild. Her parents let her paint it in shades of green and blue—like water. Her window has small panes of blue and green stained glass. When the sun shines through, you feel like you're in the middle of an aquarium.

On one wall is floor-to-ceiling shelves for her "collection." Ariel loves collecting things and can't bear to throw anything away—just like Princess Ariel. Her room is hardly ever neat, but it's interesting and fun, like Ariel herself.

"Oh, Yukiko," said Isabelle. "I looked in my mirror, but

all I saw was an adorable baby wrapped in a white blanket. I couldn't tell if it was a boy or a girl." Isabelle has a magic mirror that sometimes helps her see what might happen.

"Thanks for trying, anyway," I said.

"The most important thing is that the baby's healthy, right?" said Ella. "That's what my aunt says."

"Yeah." I sighed. "I know that's true. But I just have to get a sister! Have to, have to, have to!"

"After all . . ." Paula began.

I grinned, knowing what was coming. "Girls rule, boys drool!" we said together. I fell over laughing on Ariel's bed.

"Okay, now for the gifts!" said Ariel. She jumped up and opened her closet door, almost spilling Jasmine's punch.

"Watch that flipper, Ariel," Jasmine warned.

"I get gifts, too?" I asked excitedly.

"More for the baby," said Ella. "But you can open them."

"Twist my arm," I said, bouncing on Ariel's bed. See what I mean about the DGs being the best friends in the world?

35

I started ripping open packages. Paula had made a small book that said WELCOME, BABY. Inside she had drawn pictures of her favorite animals. "Way cool," I said.

Jasmine had bought an adorable pair of baby socks with lace on them. "More cat socks," I joked. "Great!" My friends laughed.

Ella had made a tape of herself singing lullabies—she has a terrific voice. "Perfect!" I said. "If only I could use this on the Dwarfs—to put them to sleep."

Isabelle had bought a book of nursery rhymes. "It'll be fun, reading them to her," I said.

And Ariel had made the baby a fish mobile to hang over the crib. "I'm shocked," I said. "Fish! From Ariel."

She giggled and tossed some popcorn at me.

"It's beautiful," I told her. "Thank you all so much. I can't wait to show these to Mom."

Ariel stood up and clapped her hands. "Okay, enough shower," she said. "Now, sleepover. You know there's going to be a haunted house over at Willow Green? Maybe we should all go."

"Yeah, I'll go," said Jasmine.

"Me, too," said Paula.

"Sure," said Isabelle.

"Um, actually," Ella said, "I don't really like haunted houses. They're too creepy for me."

I was relieved she said that—it hadn't sounded fun to me, either. "You guys can go if you want," I said. "But I'll hang out and keep Ella company." Ella smiled at me.

"No, we don't have to go," said Paula. "I'd rather us all do something together. Okay, guys?"

Jasmine, Isabelle, and Ariel nodded.

Since they had given in on the haunted house so easily, I decided to bring up trick-or-treating again.

"I've been thinking," I said. "Do we *really* want to go trick-or-treating? It's kind of babyish, don't you think? It's for little kids."

My five friends gave me blank looks.

"Yukiko," said Ariel patiently. "Have you forgotten about the *candy*?" Jasmine, Isabelle, Ella, and Paula nodded.

"Oh, well, okay," I said lamely. Maybe it won't be so bad, I thought. After all, I was eight now—a third grader. I would be with all my friends, and with Dr. Ramos. It would probably be a lot of fun. Everyone said so. I just wished I believed them.

Chapter Seven

Think Pink!

"Look, Jasmine bought these adorable socks," I said to Mom, holding them up. It was after dinner, and I was showing Mom all the neat stuff my friends had gotten for my new sister.

"Cat socks! Wonderful," said Mom, and we laughed together. Actually, I love cats, and so does Mom. We have four cats of our own: Perfection, Shaday, Timbalie, and Mr. Hotstuff. They're all purebred Abyssinians. Mom and Jim breed them sometimes, and then they have heart-breakingly cute kittens. Then we sell the kittens, and I get all upset. Then I get over it.

"These gifts are lovely," Mom said, getting up. "I'll be sure to thank everyone when I see them next. Now, I'm going to go take a warm bath."

"Okay." After Mom left, I hung out in my room for a while. I imagined what it would look like with a crib in it. I knew at first the baby would sleep in a bassinet in Mom and Jim's room. But soon it would be old enough to move out.

It's not an it, I told myself. *Quit thinking like that. It's a she. I mean, she's a she. Always call her that. And maybe it will come true.*

I sighed. I knew the baby was already either a boy or a girl. But I just had to believe she was a girl. A girl! I hugged myself. It would be so fantastic to have a sister! When the baby was five, I would be . . . thirteen. I could take her shopping! She could hang out with me and my friends! We would ignore my brothers together!

I sighed again. It wasn't that I hated my brothers. I didn't. In fact, I loved them all. It's just that they were so loud and rough and dirty. All of them, even Yoshi and Nobuo and Daniel, who are kind of the nicest ones. After all, I already had *six* of them. I just didn't need another boy in my life. But I desperately needed a girl.

Would the magic come through for me? Was it my destiny to finally have a sister of my own?

Well, I couldn't just sit around, waiting to see what would happen. I had to take action somehow. I knew Mom had been planning on getting down the bassinet and baby clothes soon. Maybe I could help her.

I found the bassinet up in the attic. It was wrapped in an old sheet to keep the dust out. When the twins had been born, they'd been so small that they had shared it. I had slept in this same bassinet, and so had Yoshi. Soon, my newest sibling would sleep in it, too.

I decided to make her feel right at home. Out in the garage I found a can of pink spray paint that Ben had used for a school project a few weeks ago. There was still plenty left. I dusted off the bassinet and made sure it was clean and dry. I spread old newspapers down on the ground and put the bassinet on them. Inside the house, I could hear Mom and Jim calling the boys for baths and bed. (I get to stay up a little later, because I'm the oldest.) It takes both Mom and Jim to wrangle six boys through a bath and into pajamas. Sometimes I help with Daniel or the twins. But tonight I was busy.

The spray paint worked very well. Sometimes it dripped a little, but I wiped up the drips with a rag. I sprayed the whole thing, inside and out. It was a pretty shade of pale pink. To tell you the truth, I wasn't sure Mom and Jim would approve of what I was doing. But I felt I was doing the right thing. Every single thing I did to help make the baby be a girl just had to be okay. Mom and Jim really wanted a girl, too, didn't they?

Soon I was done. I placed the pink bassinet gently behind our recycling bin and put the paint back where I got it. I decided to surprise Mom with the bassinet right after she got home from the hospital with my new sister. She would be so surprised and pleased. I hoped.

"Yukiko!" my mom called.

I was in my room on Monday afternoon, doing my homework. I had been in the family room, trying to watch my favorite nature show, but then the Dwarfs had come home. Ben and Michael decided to build a cave out of sofa cushions, Kazuo had changed the channel to some dumb cartoon he's not even supposed to watch, and Daniel had climbed up on the coffee table, then slipped off, hit his head, and started crying. That was it. After

Mom came in to comfort Daniel, I headed for my own private, quiet room, where there are No Boys Allowed.

Now it was almost dinnertime. I had heard Jim come home a little while ago. I shut my door behind me and went to see what Mom wanted.

Mom and Jim were in the kitchen. The pink bassinet was on the kitchen counter.

Uh-oh, I thought. That was quick. I guess I wasn't going to be able to surprise Mom with it after all. At least, not when she got home from the hospital.

"Yukiko, did you do this?" Mom asked. She did not look pleased.

"Yes," I said. I got the feeling that my great idea had really been kind of stupid.

Mom and Jim looked at each other.

"Honey, this bassinet was not yours to paint," said my mom. "I liked it the way it was before."

"I'm sorry," I said in a small voice.

"Also," said Jim gently, "we don't know if we're having a boy or a girl. The ultrasound on Wednesday may tell us, but it may not. We know you really want a girl, and we understand that. But the fact is, we may very well have another boy. Painting things pink isn't going to change that."

I was so embarrassed. Usually it's my brothers who have to have these little talks with Mom and Jim. Not me. Suddenly I felt like not knowing if the baby was a boy or a girl was taking over my whole life!

"I'm sorry," I said again. "I guess I can't unpaint it."

"No," said Mom. "If we have a boy, I'll paint it another color, like green, or maybe yellow. But please do not paint something that is not yours again. Okay?"

Mom didn't mean, "Is that okay with you?" She meant, "Do you understand that I'll be angry if you do this again?"

"Yeah," I said. I shuffled back to my room and threw myself facedown on my bed. Why had I done that? What a dumb idea. I pressed my face into my pillow. "I need a sister," I whispered.

Chapter Eight

And the Baby Is . . .

On Wednesday morning, before I left to catch the school bus, I gave my mom an extra hug. "Good luck, Mom," I told her. "I hope we get good news."

She hugged me back. "Yukiko, I want you to remember that as long as we find out the baby's developing normally and looks healthy, that's good news," she said seriously.

"I know," I said. "I know. It's just that—"

"Honey, we don't know what the baby will be," my mom interrupted me. "But I know I'll be happy, whatever it is. And it would be best if you made up your mind to do the same."

"Okay." I breathed out. I guess Mom had gotten a little tired of my begging her to have a girl. "I know we just want a healthy baby."

"Thank you, honey. Now run along, so you won't be late."

"I hung orange and black crepe paper streamers in the family room," Ariel told us at lunch on Wednesday. I was hardly listening. "Mom bought some fake spiderwebs and I draped them down the front stairs. It looks awesome."

It sounded great, but I could barely pay attention.

"Yukiko, what's with you today?" Isabelle asked. "You seem so far away. Do you feel all right?"

"Yes," I said. "It's just that my mom is having the ultrasound today. We might find out what the baby is."

"Whoa," said Jasmine. "Good luck."

"Thanks," I said. "I've got my fingers crossed. And I made another magic wish by the wishing well this morning. But I can't think about anything else." Ella and I met eyes. She could tell what I was thinking, how worried I was. She gave me a smile.

"It'll be okay, no matter what," she said.

I nodded and pushed my lunch away. "Let's talk about something else," I said. "To take my mind off it."

"Okay. Is everyone's costume ready?" asked Paula.

"Yep," Isabelle said. "You know, I've never even seen your fancy costumes before."

We all have Disney princess costumes. My mom helped me make mine last year, and it still fits. It's so beautiful, and it looks exactly like Snow White's dress in the movie.

"Mine is ready," I said. "We're wearing them to school on Friday, right?"

"Right," said Ella. "Everyone will be dressed up."

Just then Kenny McIlhenny passed our table on his way to stack his lunch tray. Kenny's in fourth grade, and a real pain. He lives next door to Isabelle, and she calls him the Beast.

"Hey, kids," said Kenny, staring at us. "Why are you all wearing those witches' masks? Halloween isn't till Friday."

Isabelle's eyes narrowed. "We didn't want *you* to stick out too much," she said sweetly.

"Very funny," he growled. "Just don't look in a mirror—you might break it." He stomped off to meet his friends.

"Good one, Isabelle," Jasmine said.

"He's such a weenie." Isabelle rolled her eyes.

By the time lunch was over, I knew that Mom and Jim probably had their answer. Soon I would find out. Soon all my waiting and hoping and wishing would be over.

That afternoon I actually beat Ben and Yoshi into the house. I pushed past them, raced up the walk, and flung the door open.

Mom was waiting for us in the kitchen. She was smiling.

"What? What?" I practically shrieked.

"You'll be glad to hear that our new baby looks perfectly healthy and normal in every way," Mom said. "The doctor said it seems a bit big for this stage, but it's nothing to worry about."

"Oh, good," said Ben, reaching for an apple.

"Can I go outside?" Yoshi asked, taking a glass of milk.

I felt as if I was about to explode. "Mother, what *is it*?"

Mom came over and put a hand on my shoulder. She took a deep breath. "Actually, honey, it was a little hard to tell."

I almost fell over. *"What?"*

Mom shrugged. "Ultrasounds aren't like TV," she explained. "It's not crystal clear. The baby was moving this way and that, and it was kind of hard to tell. But—" she looked at me. "The doctor thought the baby is probably a boy."

I stared at Mom.

"All right!" cried Ben. He did a little victory dance around the kitchen. "One more for the boys' team!"

"It's okay, Yuki," said Yoshi. "Us boys aren't so bad, are we?"

I burst into tears and ran to my room.

"Wow," said Paula quietly.

Of course my friends had all been waiting for me on the playground Thursday morning. I had called Ella on Wednesday night to tell her the news. She had called everyone else.

"Gee," said Jasmine. "I'm sorry."

"It's okay," I said. "Mom and I had a long talk, and I feel better about it now. Maybe it'll be a really *nice* boy."

"Yeah," said Ella. "I'm sure it will."

"Anyway," I said. "At least I know now. I don't have to worry about it anymore. This weekend I'm going to buy some paint and repaint the bassinet." I had told my friends all about the bassinet fiasco.

"Green is a good color," said Ariel. "Or blue."

"Yeah," I said. I smiled, trying to look as if I meant it.

In a way, I felt relieved that I knew the baby was a boy. Now I could relax and accept it. Deep down, I had always kind of suspected that I would end up with a new brother. And you know what? I had decided that my brothers were okay. Most of the time.

Chapter Nine

Mom and Me

When I got home from school on Thursday, Mom was sitting on my bed.

"Hi," I said. I put down my backpack.

She smiled at me.

"I guess I get to keep my very own room," I said, trying to sound cheerful.

"Probably," Mom agreed. "But you know, the doctor was not at all sure. She *thought* the baby was a boy, but it isn't one hundred percent definite. So don't get your hopes up, but don't be completely crushed yet, either."

I nodded. "Okay."

I saw Mom rubbing her hand over her stomach. It looked like a basketball under her dress.

I sat down next to her and she put her arm around my shoulders. I could hear Ben and Yoshi eating their snack in the kitchen. They were laughing about something.

"You know, I love having a daughter," said Mom. "If I didn't have at least one daughter, I would be very disappointed. And if I didn't have at least one son, I would be disappointed, too. But I have both, so I'm very lucky. The most important thing is that we're all together."

I nodded.

"Listen, can you help me for a while?" Mom asked. "I wanted to get down some baby things from the attic. I should have done it sooner—don't want to wait till the last minute."

"Sure," I said, feeling important.

We climbed up the stairs to the attic.

"Jim will have to get this crib down," said Mom. "But not for a while. Here are some boxes of baby clothes. Let's carry these down and sort them out."

In the kitchen, we could watch Ben and Yoshi playing outside. Mom fixed us a snack of apple with peanut butter, and iced tea.

Then we opened box after box. Most of the baby clothes were boy clothes, of course. Some of them were too worn to be reused. We put those in one stack. Mom made another stack of boys' clothes in good shape that she would wash. The third stack was of my old baby clothes. They didn't look worn at all.

I held up a tiny outfit with pink teddy bears on it. "I can't believe I used to fit in this," I giggled. "It looks like doll clothes."

"I know," said Mom. "You were such a lovely baby. I used to enjoy dressing you up. I was so proud of you, my first baby." She smiled at me. "I still am."

I smiled and blushed.

We put the girl clothes in another pile to be washed.

"Just in case," Mom said. "You know, soon Grandma and Grandpa will be here. They're closing up their house in Miami next week."

"It'll be fun having them here all the time," I said. I love my grandma and grandpa. They're always ready to help or play with us or read to us or do art projects with us. (I never knew my dad's parents, because they died before I was born.) Jim's mother, Grammy, is really great, too.

"It will be a huge help," Mom agreed. "It will be wonderful to have Ma helping with laundry and cooking and looking after all you children. And Jim will appreciate Pa's help in the yard."

"Yes," I said.

"Maybe then you'll have more time to see your friends and play," said Mom. "Instead of having to help so much around here."

I looked at her. "What do you mean?"

"I feel bad sometimes, knowing how much you help me," Mom said gently. "Like this morning, you put a load of clothes in the washer before school. And you empty the dishwasher almost every day. You're always doing something for the boys—helping with homework or tying shoes or helping to find something they lost. I think maybe it's too much for a girl your age."

I tried to stand up taller, to look older. "No it isn't," I said. "Everyone should try to do his or her share. You and Jim do more than any of us."

"Well, maybe we will all be able to do a little less when Ma and Pa get here," said Mom. "I just want you to know that I appreciate how much you help. I don't know what I would do without you. You're so responsible and mature."

Mom gave me a hug and a kiss. I could hardly get my arms around her, because of her huge stomach.

What she said made me feel good. But I knew that I wasn't so mature. If I were really mature, I would be able to tell my friends how I felt about trick-or-treating.

Chapter Ten

Friday the 31st

When I woke up on Friday morning, I felt both excited and worried. I was excited because I would wear my Snow White dress to school, and I always love wearing it and looking like my real self. The party at school would be terrific, too. But I still hadn't come up with a solution to my problem.

Before school Mom helped me curl my straight black hair, to make me look even more like Snow White. Then I got into my dress. I looked great.

"Mom, remember the last time I went trick-or-treating, and I got lost?" I asked.

"How could I forget?" my mom said, speaking through the bobby pins in her mouth. "I was frantic."

"Well, I haven't been trick-or-treating since then. And I'm not sure I want to go tonight," I told her.

"All your friends are going, aren't they?" Mom asked, pinning my last curl in place.

I nodded. "And Dr. Ramos will be with us. But I still think it would weird me out, going again."

"Hmm." Mom met my eyes in the mirror. "It seems like it should be a good time to try again, since you'll be with all your friends. But if you don't feel like going, just tell the girls the truth. They'll understand, because they're your friends. Come home after school, have dinner here, and go to Ariel's house when they get back. It's not a big deal."

What Mom was saying made sense, but I still felt like a sissy.

"Okay. I'll think of something," I mumbled. In the mirror, I saw Mom press her hand to her side and make a face. "Are you okay?" I asked. "Is something wrong?"

"No." Mom smiled wryly. "Aches and pains are part of being pregnant. I'm fine."

* * *

One by one my friends joined me on the school bus. They all looked amazing. Isabelle really did look like Belle. Paula looked exactly like Pocahontas. Ella had never seemed more like Cinderella. And Ariel always looks like Ariel, so that was nothing new. I wish we could dress this way all the time.

When we got to school, Jasmine was waiting for us. She was wearing her very fanciest Jasmine costume—the aqua-colored one with the gold chains and bangles sewn all over it. She looked awesome.

"Greetings, loyal subjects," she said grandly.

We laughed and bowed low. "Your Highness," we said back. A tingle of excitement went up my spine. The Disney Girls were together, we were in our favorite outfits, and we were looking forward to a party at school. I would worry about trick-or-treating later.

"Aren't you going to finish your sandwich?" I asked Ariel at lunchtime.

She shook her head. "Gotta save room for party food."

"Look, you guys," said Ella. She pulled a sheet of paper out of her lunch bag. "I've plotted the best trick-or-treating route around Willow Hill. We'll hit not only our five houses, but a bunch of other homes that always give out lots of candy. See?" she said eagerly, spreading out the map. "We'll start here, at Point A, at six-fifteen."

I couldn't help smiling. It was so—Ella. Ella is the most organized person I know. It's because for most of her life she lived alone with her dad. Since she didn't have a mother, she had to learn to keep everything going by herself.

"It'll be totally dark by then," Ella continued. "By following this route, we'll reach Point B by six-twenty-seven—that's allowing three minutes per house. Now, at Point C, maybe we should split up, to cover more houses. Yukiko, Jasmine, and I could take route 1A, and then—"

It was now or never. "I forgot to tell you guys," I blurted. "I don't think I'm going trick-or-treating tonight. Sorry."

Five Disney Girls looked at me in surprise. On Ella's face I saw confusion, and also a little bit of hurt. Why hadn't I told her? I didn't know what else to say. So I scooped up my lunch trash and walked quickly out to the playground.

Chapter Eleven

Snow White's Secret

Outside, I went to my favorite spot under the big pine tree. My friends and I like to sit in its shade and talk when it's too hot to run around. I knew that the Disney Girls deserved an explanation for my weird behavior. That is, if they were still speaking to me. I buried my head in my arms. I had really goofed.

Soft footfalls sounded near me. Moments later, someone put her hand on my arm.

"Tell me what's going on," Ella said.

I looked up. Paula, Ariel, Jasmine, and Isabelle were

59

headed our way. They sat in a circle around me, concerned expressions on their faces.

"I've been so stupid," I said. "I didn't know how to tell you. And I don't want to be a party pooper. But I've decided I don't want to go trick-or-treating."

"We know," said Ariel impatiently. "We got it. But I don't get *why*."

I let out a heavy sigh. "It's kind of stupid."

"If it's how you feel, then it isn't stupid," Paula said.

"Well, when I was five," I began, "I went trick-or-treating with my mom, Yoshi, and the twins."

"Where was I?" asked Ella.

"We didn't go together that year," I reminded her.

"Oh, right," she said. "I went with my dad."

"Anyway," I continued, "the twins were just a year old, in their stroller. This was when we lived over on Linnet Place. Trick-or-treating was a lot of fun—at first. Then all of a sudden, we noticed that Yoshi was missing."

"Uh-oh," said Paula.

"Mom and I called him, but we didn't see him anywhere. I thought maybe he was back at the last house, so I ran back to look for him. But he wasn't there, so I ran back to the house before that." I shrugged my shoulders.

"What happened was, *I* got lost. Yoshi turned up right away—he hadn't wandered far after all. But I got totally confused in the dark, and I was all turned around. Before I even realized it, I couldn't see Mom anywhere. I called and called her, but she couldn't hear me."

"You must have been so scared," said Ella.

I nodded. "I was. I waited a long time, but Mom didn't come. All these older kids dressed in scary costumes went by me, and they kept leaning over to say *'Boo!'* really loud. The dark trees rustled overhead in a spooky way. I started to imagine that ghosts and goblins and witches were about to jump on me. I mean, I was only five."

"Yeah, of course," said Isabelle.

"I think I would have started crying," said Paula.

"I did," I admitted. "Finally I just sat down on the street curb and started bawling. Right away, a man came up and asked what was wrong. I told him what my mom looked like. The man and his kids looked for Mom, and found her around the corner, a block away."

"That was so nice of him," said Paula.

"I was so relieved when my mom ran up," I said. "Anyway, since then, I haven't gone trick-or-treating," I finished. "I guess it's pretty stupid, huh? I mean, I'm eight now. And we would be all together. I just don't think it sounds fun. I'd rather just stay home and hand out candy to other kids."

"Why didn't you tell us?" Ella asked. "We kept talking about trick-or-treating, and you never told us how you felt."

"I didn't want you to think I was such a big baby," I admitted. "And I've been all caught up with finding out whether the baby was a boy or a girl. The time never seemed right."

Ella sighed in that patient way she has. "Yu-ki-ko." She sounded like she was trying to explain something to a dog. "This is *us* you're talking to. *Us.* The Disney Girls. Don't you know you can tell us *anything?*"

I nodded, feeling a little embarrassed.

"Geez, if you can't tell us, who could you tell?" Ariel demanded. "We're your best friends."

"Yeah," said Jasmine. "I mean, we *are* the Disney Girls. We're special. We have to stick together no matter what."

"Thanks," I mumbled, feeling a little shy.

"Look," said Ariel. "No biggie. We'll pick you up to go to my house after we're done trick-or treating. Okay?"

I smiled happily. "Deal."

Chapter Twelve

A Halloween Surprise

We had two classes after lunch, before we could begin our class party. I was so psyched that I couldn't concentrate at all. What a weight off my shoulders! I was so thankful that my friends had understood.

At last, Ms. Timmons looked at the clock, put down her textbook, and went to knock on Mr. Murchison's door. We all leaped up.

Minutes later, Mr. Murchison's whole class filed into our classroom—including Paula, Jasmine, and Isabelle.

"Happy Halloween!" I called to them. I meant it, too!

The two teachers started getting the refreshments ready.

I had brought a tray of sugar cookies that Mom and I had decorated to look like jack-o'-lanterns. There were also bowls of punch, chips and dip, orange-and-chocolate cupcakes, and tons of other stuff.

Ms. Timmons had brought her portable CD player and Kenny McIlhenny put on a CD of scary sounds. He grinned as a wolf howl pierced the air.

Isabelle rolled her eyes. "The Beast strikes again."

Terry Bock, dressed as Frankenstein, held his arms out straight and started lurching across the room. Alan Hill and Eric Morgenstein, from fourth grade, started howling like wolves, too, along with the CD. Jason Heidenberger and Barclay Forbes, from our class, grinned at us. They were wearing vampire fangs.

The Disney Girls looked at each other and sighed.

"As we said, girls rule, boys drool," said Jasmine.

"That's the sad truth," said Isabelle.

Finally Rebecca James changed the CD and put on one that had fun Halloween songs, like "Monster Mash." Ariel started dancing, then Paula joined her, and soon half of the kids at the party were hopping around Ms. Timmons's classroom.

It was a terror-ific party.

I was bummed when the three o'clock bell rang and school was over. I wish we could have a class party every single week! But we gathered up our book bags and headed outside to the school buses.

"Okay," I said, slinging my backpack up on my shoulder. "So I'll see you guys around seven-thirty—assuming you keep to your strict schedule. Just think of me as Point Z."

The others laughed and Ella punched me lightly in the arm.

"I can't help it if I'm organized," she said.

"See you later, Yukiko," called Ben. He and Yoshi were going to their friend's house, so they were taking a different bus.

"Have fun tonight," I called to them. They were both hyped up about going trick-or-treating. Ben was going to be a mummy, and Yoshi was a samurai.

I climbed on the bus after Paula. Jasmine was excited to be riding with us instead of driving home with her mom.

Then Paula said, "Yukiko—isn't that your mom's minivan?" She pointed out the window.

I looked, and it *was* Mom's minivan, pulling up in

front of our bus! I jumped off the bus and hurried over to it.

Jim rolled down the driver's window. "Yukiko!" he said. "Hop into the van! I'm taking Mom to the hospital! The baby's coming!"

My mouth dropped open in a surprised O. Then I looked at Mrs. Holiday, our school bus driver, and she waved at me to go. (She needs a parent's permission to let you *not* ride the bus home.)

"Bye, guys!" I yelled to the Disney Girls. They were all hanging out the windows, looking thrilled and excited and a little worried.

"Call us later!" Ariel yelled back. I nodded, then ran back and leaped into the minivan. I had scarcely buckled myself into the backseat when Jim pulled out quickly from the curb.

"Careful, sweetheart," my mom said to him. "Let's not have an accident. We have plenty of time. I think."

"Sorry, sorry," Jim muttered, looking at the traffic in his rearview mirror.

I stared at my mom, feeling stunned. At last, the day was here! My newest brother had decided to make an early appearance!

"Mom, are you all right?" I asked anxiously.

She turned around. She was blowing out deep breaths, as if she was running. But she stopped for a moment to smile at me. "Yes, I'm fine," she said, sounding short of breath. "But surprised! The baby's two weeks early. Uh-oh." She sat back and gripped Jim's free hand for a minute, her eyes shut.

"Mom?" Why weren't we at the hospital yet?

Mom opened her eyes and breathed out deeply. "Whew," she said. She reached her hand back and I leaned forward to hold it. "Your brothers are all with friends or neighbors," Mom told me. "We called Grandma and Grandpa, and they're on their way from Miami. Uh-oh." She leaned back and closed her eyes again, taking deep breaths. She was squeezing my hand so hard I thought I felt my bones crunching.

"Hang on, sweetheart," said Jim tensely. "We're almost there. You okay?"

Mom breathed out. "I'm okay," she said. She turned back to smile at me. "This is exciting, isn't it?"

I nodded, my eyes huge. It was exciting and kind of scary. I actually didn't even remember my mom having the twins—I had been only four years old, and I think my dad took me and Yoshi to the zoo that day. I had never seen it happening before.

"Uh-oh." Mom leaned back again. Jim glanced at his watch.

"They're only three minutes apart." He sounded worried. "But here we are at the hospital! Okay, Yukiko—let's get her inside."

Chapter Thirteen

And Sleepy Makes Seven

Jim parked the minivan. He helped Mom out of the front seat. I was so nervous I tried to leap out of the car without unfastening my seat belt!

"Shouldn't we get a stretcher or something?" I asked as I ran up to Mom and put my arm around her waist.

Mom laughed. "I can walk," she assured me. "I'm not sick—I'm just having a baby. Women do this all the time. And remember, this is my fifth one. Piece of cake."

That calmed me down a little. With Jim on one side and me on the other, Mom walked slowly to the admitting room.

Minutes later, we were settling Mom into a birthing room. It looked just like a hotel room, except it had some medical equipment attached to one wall.

"Hello, Mrs. Hayashi," said a nurse, bustling in with sheets and a hospital gown. "I'm Cathy, your nurse. Esther is on her way." Esther is my mom's nurse/midwife. That's someone who specializes in delivering babies. Mom also had a doctor to help, but she told me the midwife would probably take care of everything.

Cathy looked at me, standing by my mom's bed, still holding her hand. "Hi, Snow White!" she said cheerfully. "I see that your mom has a special helper."

I almost fell over from shock—how had she recognized me? Then I realized I was still wearing my Snow White costume for Halloween! I giggled and nodded.

Another nurse bustled in. Jim and I stepped back while they made Mom comfortable in a hospital gown, and put on her wrist tag. Mom kept having to stop and take deep breaths.

When the nurses left, Jim and I each held one of Mom's hands as she sat up in bed. Sometimes she squeezed really hard, but neither Jim nor I complained. We just wanted to help.

"I'm so glad you're both here," Mom said in between breaths. "I remember when you were born," she told me. "I was so thrilled. You were the most beautiful baby."

"Does it hurt?" I asked timidly.

"Yes," Mom admitted. "But not like an injury. More like your body's trying really hard to do something. And you know you can look forward to holding the baby afterward, so you don't mind so much. Uh-oh." She lay back against the bed and breathed deeply.

Soon Esther, the midwife, came in. She smiled at me, then examined Mom. "Wow, you're going to have this baby soon!" she said, sounding pleased. "You're almost ready, and you're doing a good job."

"Thanks," Mom said, closing her eyes again.

"Sweetie," Jim said to me, "maybe it's time for you to wait for us outside."

"Okay," I said shakily. I kissed Mom and she hugged me.

"See you soon," she promised.

Outside, the waiting area was very comfortable. There were several other people waiting. I settled into a deep chair. The nurse, Cathy, brought me a soda. I tried to read a magazine, but couldn't. From down the hall, I heard a baby crying, but it wasn't our baby. Every minute felt like an hour.

A new baby. A new brother. Mom had said it wasn't one hundred percent definite, but I had made up my mind to accept another boy. All along, I had wanted a girl so much. Now I realized how worried I was. The baby wasn't even supposed to be born until the middle of November. Would it be all right?

I checked to make sure no one was looking. Then I held my magic heart charm tightly in my hand. Right there in the waiting room, I closed my eyes and made a silent secret wish:

All the magic powers that be,
Hear me now, my special plea.
I know that you can help my mother—
Please also help my newest brother.

I felt my charm grow warm in my hand—a sign that the magic was working. I relaxed a bit. After all, I was in my Snow White dress, holding my charm: I knew the magic had heard me.

"Yukiko!" Jim burst through the waiting room door, a huge smile on his face. I jumped up and ran to him. We hugged each other. "Your mom is terrific. Come see the baby," said Jim.

Inside the birthing room, Mom seemed tired. Her face was pink and her hair needed brushing. But she looked really happy. I knew everything was fine and silently I thanked the magic for coming through again.

In Mom's arms was a tiny bundle wrapped in a white blanket. I leaned close and saw a pale little face with small, smushed features and a wet cap of fine black hair. Two weensy fists were curled beneath the chin. He looked like a boy. This was my new brother, after so many months of waiting. Here was the seventh Dwarf.

"He's beautiful," I said. I touched the tiny fist. "What's his name?"

Mom and Jim smiled at me. Mom touched the baby's cheek. "Her name is Suzue," she said. (She pronounced it Soo-zoo-ay.) "Suzie for short."

I felt my eyes get wide. Suzie? I grabbed my heart charm and jumped up and down. "A sister!" I cried. "I have a sister!"

Chapter Fourteen

Trick-or-Treat

Yep. She was a girl. The ultrasound just hadn't been clear enough for them to really tell. It was the best surprise any of us had ever had in our entire lives.

Jim and I stayed with Mom and Suzie for another hour. Then Mom really needed to rest, and the baby did, too. (It's hard work, being born.) We kissed Mom and Suzie good-bye.

"I'll be back as soon as things at home are settled," Jim promised.

"Bye, Mom," I said. Then I leaned close to whisper, "I told my friends the truth. They understood. Everything is okay."

Her dark eyes lit up and she squeezed my hand. "I'm so glad."

"Ouch," I said, pulling my hand away. "It still hurts."

When Jim and I got home, my grandma and grandpa were just pulling up in a taxi. I ran to them and told them the wonderful news. Grandma clapped her hands in joy, and Grandpa slapped Jim on the back so hard Jim's glasses almost fell off.

The next hour was very hectic. We called all my brothers' friends and told my brothers to come home. It still wasn't even dinnertime yet! It felt like about ten o'clock at night. But it was dark, and Jim ordered in a couple of large pizzas with everything.

When the Dwarfs got home, Jim let me tell them about our new sister. They were almost as pleased as I was.

"I guess one more sister won't be so bad," said Ben. "I mean, *you're* okay."

I gave him a hug. He made a face and pushed me away.

Grandpa had brought a bottle of champagne, and my grandparents and Jim toasted little Suzie as we ate pizza.

Throughout everything, our doorbell rang nonstop. Ben and I took turns running to the door to hand out candy to the trick-or-treaters. I was so thrilled about my new sister that I gave everyone double portions.

With everything that was going on, I *almost* forgot about the Disney Girl sleepover! In the middle of a bite of pizza, I remembered to look at the clock. It was almost seven-thirty!

"Oh, my gosh!" I exclaimed. "My friends will be here any minute!" Probably *exactly* at seven-thirty, if I knew Ella.

Jim grinned. "They can help us celebrate. Are you packed for the sleepover?"

"Yes," I said. Then I got an idea. "I bet they're working their way up our street right now. Can I run out to find them?"

"Sure." Jim stood up. "I'll go with you. Dai, Akako, can you hold the fort?" (Dai is my grandfather's name. It means "big." Akako is my grandmother. Her name means "red," which is a lucky color.)

"Sure, no problem," said Grandpa.

I ran out into the night. The streetlights made everything glow like magic. Our street was lined with small groups of kids dressed for Halloween, and their parents. I saw a small dragon, a Dalmatian puppy, a fairy princess, and a daisy. They looked like they were having fun.

Suddenly I spotted my friends: five girls, each dressed as her favorite Disney princess. Dr. Ramos, Ariel's dad, was following a few feet behind them.

"Guys! Guys!" I yelled, waving my arms.

They saw me and started running over. As soon as they were close enough, I shouted, "It's a girl! I have a sister!"

Ella stopped in her tracks and dropped her plastic pumpkin full of treats. "Oh, my gosh!" she yelled, jumping up and down. "Oh, my gosh!" We grabbed each other, hugging and twirling in a circle.

"A girl!" said Ariel. She punched the sky. "All right!"

Gasping for breath, I quickly told my friends about being at the hospital, and finding out I had a sister, and everything.

"And you know what?" I leaned closer to them and

whispered. "It was the magic. The magic helped every-thing work out perfectly."

My friends nodded. They'd seen magic work before.

"Hey, wait a minute," Ella said. "Here you are—it's Halloween, and everyone's out trick-or-treating. Do you think you want to give it a try?"

I looked around. I was on a brightly lit street, with familiar houses everywhere. Jim was with me, and all my friends, and Dr. Ramos. Trick-or-treating suddenly seemed like a good idea!

"After all," Isabelle said, "your new sister was born on Halloween. That means it can't be all bad."

I laughed and nodded. "There's one other really great thing that happened on Halloween," I told them. "When I told you the story about my getting lost, I never men-tioned the best part: the man who rescued me that night was *Jim*. That's how he and my mom met. You might say I brought them together—on Halloween."

"You're kidding!" said Jasmine. "That's incredible!"

"Now, three years later, he's your stepfather, and you have a brand-new baby sister," marveled Ella. "Talk about magic!"

I beamed at my friends. A lot of wonderful things had

happened since that Halloween when I was five. Right then, I made a decision. I picked up Ella's plastic pumpkin, marched up to my neighbor's house, and rang the doorbell.

"Trick-or-treat!" I called.

"And now, for our sugarplums," said Mademoiselle Sandra, consulting her notebook. "Ah, yes. We will begin with Ariel." She smiled at me and reached behind her to the rack. I leaped forward, ready to take my costume. She pulled out a hanger and handed it to me. My heart pounded. It was shiny and plum colored, with a tutu . . . wait. No tutu.

"Um, Mademoiselle?" I asked, examining my hanger. "Is there a part missing? My skirt?"

"No," she said, looking my costume over. "No, my dear, it is all here." She smiled again.

I slanted my head this way and that, trying to figure out what I was seeing on the hanger. It wasn't a tutu. It wasn't a dress, or a tunic. It looked—big. Too big. It looked wierd.

"See," said Mademoiselle Sandra. She must have noticed how confused I seemed. "You'll put it on—your arms go here, your legs come out here. Then we stuff the inside with netting, to make it pouf out, so . . . "

It dawned on me. I finally got it. My costume was *not* a lovely, *pretend* version of a sugarplum. My costume was a sugarplum. I would be dressed as a *great, big, round, enormous, purple berry*!!! I would look like that girl from Willie Wonka! I almost fainted as the horrible truth filtered into my shocked brain.

has Ariel made a mistake, or will she trade in her flippers for toe shoes forever?

#5 *Cinderella's Castle*

The Disney Girls are so excited about the school's holiday party. Ella decides that the perfect thing for her to make is an elaborate gingerbread castle. But creating such a complicated confection isn't easy, even for someone as super-organized as Ella. And her stepfamily just doesn't seem to understand how important this is to her. Ella could really use a fairy godmother right now . . .

#6 *One Pet Too Many*

Paula's always loved animals, any animal. Who else would have a pet raccoon, not to mention two cats, a dog, three rabbits, and countless fish? When Paula finds a lost baby armadillo, though, her parents say, "No more pets!"—and that's that. But how much trouble could a baby armadillo be? Plenty, as Paula discovers—especially when she's trying to keep it a secret from her parents.

#7 *Adventure in Walt Disney World:*
A Disney Girls Super Special

The Disney Girls are so excited. They're all going to dress up as their favorite Disney Princesses and participate in the Magic Kingdom Princess Parade. And as a special treat, Jasmine's mom is taking them to stay overnight at a hotel in the park. Magical things are bound to happen to the Disney Girls in the most magical place on earth—and they do . . .